# Table of (

# Copyright © 2024 by Hans Wrang

## Disclaimer

# Also by Hans Wrang

The Adventures of Gammelnok
A three hundred year journey to reach a garden pond
Jesper Knasfis
Be a Buddy not a Bully
The Good Life in a Hilltop Village
Village life during Franco Regime
The Azalea Murder
JK Investigates
Walking to Africa
A Stork's Journey
Childhood Memories
Growing up on a small farm in Southern Denmark

# The Tree Dwellers

A fairy tale
by
Hans Wrang

# Dedication

To my wife Hazel
She keeps coming up with
Crazy ideas
Thank you for that

# Introduction

A row of 24 Holm Oak trees line the street.
In its branches reside many Tree Dwellers of all ages.
If one is lucky to spot a Tree Dweller, the impression is
fleeting and one would question oneself if one saw
something or someone at all. Maybe it was just a
figment of one's imagination. Better to keep quiet and
not be thought of as a nutcase.
This is the story of the Tree Dwellers.

# Chapter 1: Doomsday approaches

Every eight years or so, there is a Doomsday. The next one is coming up soon. Rumors have it that the town council has put the pruning of the Holm Oak trees out to tender. That means they will have to Bunch Up - again!

Donna, a relatively young Tree Dweller is the current leader, having been in charge for just over a year. Donna has a head of long dark brown curly hair that sometimes trips her up when moving between trees. She is reluctant to have it cut, so wears her hair in a bun normally, but it is unruly at best. Her round Harry Potter-style glasses keep slipping down her nose when she talks animatedly, which is quite often.

She loves to laugh, and if you are lucky, walking the pavement on a windy night, as you pass underneath Tree Number Five you might hear her laugh up there in the branches. But can you be sure?

This Doomsday coming will be the fourth since Donna was born. She can only remember the last two and the experience was not a happy one. As the trees were pruned, one by one the Dwellers had to move up the row where it got more crowded as Doomsday crept nearer and the trees to hide in got fewer.

This year Donna seeks the advice of her mentor, friend, and predecessor, Joshua who has two Doomsdays under his belt.

They meet late one moonlit night in Tree Number Three where Joshua lives with his wife and two daughters.

"I need some advice on how to deal with our other twenty-two families over the coming weeks and possibly months when we will be exposed until the leaves start shooting again and we can get some cover. How do we escape the scrutiny of the people in this town when they can see us up here in the bare branches?"

"Do not worry, Donna," says Joshua "They will not see you. First of all, have you noticed that most people look down when they walk? That is to avoid stepping in dog droppings. Also, you know we can change our coloring to fit the background. Last Doomsday we started moving back down when the Pruners got to Tree Number Twenty. The pressure eased and we clung to our bare branches in the daytime, looking very grey but unnoticeable to the general populace. By the time they got to the last tree, we were all down the row, clinging. It took nearly a month to get back to normal, but no one knows we are here and you should just relax. Things will work out as they always do."

# Chapter 2: Disaster at Tree Number Nine

Things did not work out as Joshua had promised.

The family at Tree Number Nine refused to move when it became time to Bunch Up.

A fierce woman of little sense and a timid husband of little courage occupied Tree Number Nine. They had a bunch of small children who managed to survive by moving between trees and begging tidbits. It was impossible to tell if they were girls or boys. They were dressed almost identically in their rags.

How they had managed to get adopted into the Tribe nobody seemed to know or remember. Lowlife they were and none of the neighboring Tree Dwellers seemed to be friends of theirs.

Donna decides to call a meeting of the Elders. As pruning had only just begun, it was still safe to hold the meeting in her tree. The Elders living at the beginning of the row though had already started moving up, now residing in Tree Number Four with Diego. Midnight was approaching and the four Elders made an appearance. Joshua, Alberto, Pepe, and Diego arrived as a group, all male and all now looking at Donna from separate branches.

Donna opened the meeting, explaining that Tree Number Nine had refused to move when the Bunching Up was about to begin. This in itself was not a problem, as they may not be noticed, but if they were, all hell could break loose. The whole existence of all the Tree Dwellers may be in danger. How would they fare if the townspeople got scared, not knowing what they were up against, and started either chopping down the trees or worse, using poison to eradicate a perceived pest? No, it was essential to either persuade Tree Number Nine to comply with Tribe rules or be evicted forthwith.

Pepe, the most amicable of the Elders, volunteered to have a word the following evening during dinner.

Dinner normally consisted of catching a few Sparrows or Starlings who use Holm Oak trees for their overnight roost. Thousands fly in at dusk making a loud racket as they settle in for the night. A few eaten would not be missed.

The noise would disguise Pepe's approach. Pepe was not worried about the timid husband; he would do as told by his fierce wife. But the woman was a formidable lowlife person with a foul mouth and a temper to match.

As Pepe arrived, unannounced and unnoticed he observed the family. They were in the middle of dinner, feathers still spilling out of their mouths as they devoured small birds at leisure. No table manners observed Pepe as he sat down on a branch and confronted the family.

The message was brief and to the point: Bunch Up or leave the Tribe.

# Chapter 3: Getting Crowded

Now two weeks into pruning time the workers are reaching Tree Number Nine. Donna and her Council of Elders have long since started to Bunch Up.

At Tree Number Nine, they have observed eight families now moving through their home on the way further up the line. Each family has treated them with disdain, but urging them to move as the whole Tribe might be in danger because of their intransigence.

In the end, it was the children who managed to soften up their mother and persuade her to follow the Tribe up the line of trees.

There are no cheers at this news, just relief, and as far as Donna is concerned, a special Doomsday is waiting for that family when things settle down again later in the year.

Trees Twenty to Twenty-four are now getting exceedingly crowded and it is time to decide who should move back down the line. Whoever goes, will have to change from green to grey to blend in. They will also face several weeks if not months clinging to a bare branch, quietly resting so as not to attract attention to them being there during the daytime.

There is also the problem of food. No green foliage, no sparrows or starlings roosting. But there is a solution to that problem. Although a strange one!

# Chapter 4: Feeding the Grey

The Tree Dwellers have a special gift that has enabled them to survive close to people for decades. Living ten feet above ground gives them an unnoticeable existence. They are there but they are not there. When they do show themselves on occasion, people see them but they do not leave an impression at all.

As is the case at Grey Time, the time while they wait for the trees to start sprouting new leaves and attract their main source of food: Roosting sparrows and starlings.

Then they have no option but to slither down the trunk of their tree and venture into nearby shops, restaurants, or takeaways.

They discretely approach the counter of a takeaway for example. They have a written list of what they need or want. It is placed on the counter in front of the proprietor. No words are spoken. The order is taken to the kitchen. Nothing is entered into the till, so no records of this particular transaction.

When the food is eventually produced and handed over, the Tree Dweller exits the establishment and not only do they disappear from sight but also from the memory of the proprietor. There is no record of anything having happened, apart from the fact that the chef out back might be accused of stocktaking improprieties even though the small shortfall may never be noticed.

It is quite another matter when The Tree Dwellers try to get packets of biscuits and crisps from the local Cash-and-carry warehouse.

Maria, the proprietor is acutely aware of the poverty around her in the neighboring district. That is one reason she has started her low-cost warehouse, seeing a market for low-priced and low-quality food and day-to-day cleaning and disposable items. She is watching everything that goes into baskets along the aisles and comparing it to what is handed to her at the till. Any discrepancies are dealt with without mercy. Options like Police, Pay, or Return the Goods are offered together with the request never to return to her warehouse, ever again. They will be remembered.

How can a Tree Dweller possibly get anything out of the warehouse without Maria noticing?

Distraction! Maria is wise to that one. That will not work in her warehouse. So what will; Flattery, Sleight of Hand, Threats, or Intimidation?

Honesty! That might work. Telling Maria that it is Grey Time and they are hungry. She may have a soft spot somewhere behind that iron-clad exterior. It might work, but probably only once, and once may not be enough. Grey Time normally lasts a few months. They may starve to death before then.

So, telling an honest lie is what is called for here. Once the goods have passed the counter, she will have forgotten about them ever being there.

Maria sees them approaching the till. A father, mother, and two kids; all dressed in grey. It feels weird but they seem friendly and honest. The purchases are lined up in front of her and some untold story from her childhood is mentally presented to her; a story of hunger and poverty in her native Romania. She forgets what she is doing, passing the goods over the barcode reader and letting the family bag the goods, and she lets them leave without paying. After a while, she shakes her head and looks out the warehouse door; nobody is there. The only thing that can explain what just happened is the fact that at the next stock take, there are certain discrepancies.

# Chapter 5: Taking Tribe Members to Task

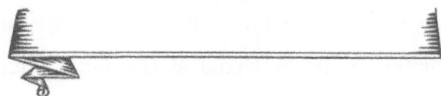

The lowlife family at Tree Number Nine needs to be taught a lesson. They had endangered the whole tribe by refusing to Bunch Up and that act cannot go unpunished. Donna has to maintain her grip on authority and her leadership capabilities cannot be challenged.

Donna has called a meeting of the Elders to help her decide what to do with the disobedience of the Dwellers in Tree Number Nine.

They meet on the last night before the new moon as has been custom since the trees were big enough to house Dwellers. Joshua, Alberto, Pepe and Diego appear on time and are dressed somberly in Dark Green as befits the severity of the situation.

Donna, dressed in dark grey opens the meeting. What should be done about the family in Tree Number Nine? The council Elders are all sensible people, not prone to overreact or voice opinions they cannot substantiate. They have all in their turn been where Donna is now. Joshua is the youngest and Pepe the oldest, spanning nearly five decades. What wisdom they have between them they are prepared to share with Donna. Integrity, honesty, and respect are the values the Elders try to instill in all their Tribe members.

As one family has decided that they do not value these sentiments and rules that would allow them a continued relationship with the rest of the Tribe, there is nothing really to debate. But debate they must. Although Donna is the leader of the Tribe and the head of the Council, she does not have the authority in a case like this, to act on her own.

They talk among themselves for not more than a few minutes when it becomes clear they are all in agreement. But first, in the name of fairness, they will have to hear what the family in Tree Number Nine has to say for themselves.

Duly summoned, first, the fierce wife appears, soon followed by her timid husband and three grubby and sullen children.

She looks defiantly at the five Elders confronting her. She can see in their eyes that the verdict is a foregone conclusion - eviction. But she is not about to go without a fight.

"Have you any idea at all what goes on in this row of trees?" She begins. "Do you know how many unhappy families there are? Are you aware that in number Twenty-Four four grown boys, their parents, and one grandparent squeeze together in a space far too small for seven Dwellers? They only have six main branches in their tree to rest on, so have to take turns; do you know that in Tree Number Eighteen the parents struggle with a sick child? As far as the family in Tree Number Twelve is concerned, they have long battled with broken bones due to malnutrition. So, your problems are far greater than one family who refuses to obey your orders to Bunch Up. You, Donna, and the rest of you are in for a surprise as soon as the leaves grow back. There is unrest brewing and maybe your grip on power will be challenged soon."

"If what you say is remotely true," Donna replies, "then I still consider you as a source of future trouble. As such, the Tribe will be better off without you. You have until tomorrow night when we have a New Moon to crawl down and move your family down into the valley below. There is a large clump of trees there which you can reach before dawn. There is plenty of space there, and I am sure you will be welcomed by the other outcasts. This decision is unanimous and not open to appeal. You have to be gone by daylight the day after tomorrow."

The family retreats but the oldest son, maybe twelve years of age, turns back as they leave and issues a specific threat to Donna. "I will remember you and I will come back and haunt you. Stay vigilant!"

# Chapter 6: Testing for Rumbles of Dissent

Autumn is fast approaching with cooler days and now lush foliage. Sparrows and starlings are returning to roost every night and food is plentiful. There are even some acorns forming. These are too hard to chew though but are collected and kept for playthings for the children. One or two of the older population even remember how to pierce holes and join up acorns to form small animals. If the stalk is still attached to the fruit itself it resembles a pipe. Small children are moving through the branches, pretending to smoke these make-believe pipes.

Donna has been visiting the populace and asking questions to gauge the level of their grievances and concerns. She finds that things are mostly calm and that the Tribe is content with the way life is treating them. There are as always complaints as to the Bunching Up during pruning time, but the discomfort is mostly forgotten now after a few months of plenty of food and lots of space in the branches.

When she gets to Tree Number Twenty-Four, the Grandparent is dying. The family is crowded around and takes it in turn to mop his brow. It will not be long now before he leaves them. As Donna and the family watch, he slips away peacefully.

Within an hour his body crumbles slowly to dust and falls through the branches onto the pavement below.

The following morning, she knows that Miguel the street sweeper will see the pile of dust, look up into the leaves above, and taking off his straw sombrero mutter to himself: 'There goes another one. Good luck to them.' He will then slowly sweep the pile of dust off the pavement onto the barren ground below. Maybe something good will grow there one day.

As Donna ends her tour of inspection at the last tree without further incidents, she turns back towards her end of the line of trees. On the way, she looks in on the family with the sick child at Tree Number Eighteen. The child is much improved, thanks to knowledgeable neighbors who are capable of using herbal medication.

It is quite a different story at Tree Number Twelve. This family still suffers broken bones due to fatigue caused by malnutrition, making it difficult for them to negotiate the branches when trying to catch sparrows or starlings. It is a downward spiral.

All though it is against the Tribe's code of conduct for survival and ethics that should always be observed to allow nature to coexist with the Tribe, Donna arranges for this family to have a small meshed net they can suspend between two branches allowing them to easier grab a few birds for their dinner. The strict arrangement is that once they recover their strength, the net will be returned to the main stores and hopefully never be used again.

Feeling that she has had a good journey across all the trees, Donna arrives back home at Tree Number Five. Looking down through the branches, she spots a young person looking up into the row of trees. Not sure if her tree is the object of attention, she is never the less disturbed by the incident. The youngster below is about the right age for one of the sons dispelled earlier in the year. On the other hand, he looks too well-dressed to be one of them. What, she worries, is such a young person doing out at this time of night staring at her tree?

# Chapter 7: Getting New Dwellers

When older dwellers turn to dust, there is a need to bring in new blood. Not an easy task. This very night though, Donna is in for a nasty surprise. A stranger knocks on her tree trunk late and announces that he is her replacement as leader of the Tree Dwellers.

He asks to be admitted and given the courtesy to explain himself. Donna could hardly refuse, her curiosity aroused and her unease at a very high level. What is going on here?

The stranger introduces himself as Don Perito, having recently arrived from a nearby province. He has been ordered here by the overall powerful council of Tree Dwellers. He is aware of the vacancy in Tree Number Nine and asks permission to take over that particular tree.

Donna is confused, both by the calmness and politeness of the newcomer but also by why she is to be replaced as leader. What has she done that cannot be condoned? Asking what will happen to her, she is informed that she will be elevated to the Council of Elders when she steps down as leader, in favor of Don Perito.

This is even more confusing as there can always only ever be four members in the Elder Council. Not to worry, says Don Perito. One will turn to dust soon.

Now Donna is really worried. One of her four friends on the Council of Elders is to die. Who will it be and why? They have known each other for many a Doomsday and she does not want to lose any one of them. What power does this so-called Don Perito hold? He has not shown her any proof of who he is, although he seems to know exactly what is going on in her row of twenty-four Holm Oaks.

"You have shown a lack of judgment, endangering the strength of the Tribe. Firstly by evicting a family where the woman dared to tell you where you failed. Secondly, allowing an ailing family to use a net to catch food to survive. Netting is strictly forbidden and that family should have been left to crumble to dust. Only the strong can be allowed to survive. The Tribe depends on it. You now have to decide which one of the four Elders has to turn to dust for you to progress."

# Chapter 8: Deciding on who has to go

Donna is in distress. She has to decide who has to live and who has to die. It is an unbelievably difficult decision to have to make. She questions if this new arrival who wants her job is a real Tree Dweller or an imposter, who with good intelligence can fool them all.

An Elder meeting is called for urgently even if they are between New and Old Moons. This is serious and Donna is determined to fight for the lives of her friends; whichever one has to be forfeited. Swearing quietly to herself she wishes a curse on Don Perito.

An informal meeting at Donna's tree around midnight is the venue. The four Elders turn up in high spirits, expecting a party get-together, not believing it is an extraordinary meeting.

Smiles all around, they settle themselves on one of the five main branches available. Looking at Donna's face, the hilarity soon evaporates and they all look at her expectantly, worry creeping onto their faces.

Donna does not let them wait long. She jumps straight into her dilemma. One of the four will have to die soon unless they can find a solution to this dangerous situation.

She explains about the stranger and unannounced visitor Don Perito who entered their domain the night before. How he has taken residence in Tree Number Nine and how he expects to take over Donna's position as soon as she is elevated to the Council of Elders. She continues her explanations, telling how this Don Perito knows about the undesirables having been expelled and how she, Donna had a family make use of netting to feed themselves.

The four Elders look at Donna, small smiles appearing on their faces. They are fully aware of the burden leadership piles on anyone's shoulders. But Donna has tried to be honest with them, and that counts for a lot. If this Don Perito is for real, they do acknowledge that a problem has indeed landed in their lap.

"I see a problem here," says Pepe. "There can only be four Elders at any one time. If you are elevated to an Elder position, one of us has to go. But how, and who should it be? Nobody has ever resigned from the Elder Council and only Death can create a vacancy." Pepe stops as the truth dawns on him. "Who is it to be?" he asks, looking at the other three Elders. "You cannot just kill one of us. And none of us are willing to crumble to dust voluntarily. We have families to look after. This Don Perito must be crazy if he thinks he can just climb up here and take over." Pepe is indignant and a little bit frightened. What if he is the one that has to forfeit his life?

Donna explains that that decision has been placed on her shoulders. Unless there is a volunteer!

# Chapter 9: Don Perito the Impostor

Don Perito is settling in quite nicely in the empty Tree Number Nine, vacated by the family Donna had expelled earlier in the year. He is looking forward to becoming the leader of this Tribe of Tree Dwellers. Ever since he was expelled from a tribe some hundreds of kilometers to the west he has harbored an intense hatred and an overwhelming desire to get his own back on the powers that be.

As he had wandered the country for a suitable target, he had stumbled into a clump of trees down the valley from this little village where he is now. There, a mixture of low-life dwellers and outcasts had sheltered him for a few days. Wasting no time digging up as much dirt as he could on the Holm Oak Dwellers, he had found an opening and he was going to exploit it to the best of his ability.

As Don Perito starts to mull over the events that eventually resulted in him being expelled from his Tribe and forced to wander the vast Spanish countryside in search of somewhere to call home once again, he recalls the events leading up to his expulsion.

He originated from the province of Extremadura, where Holm Oaks are plenty but spaced out over large areas. Black pigs would roam underneath the trees feeding on fallen acorns, fattening themselves up happily, not realizing that the more they grew, the more attractive they became to the land owner. Not attractive in a beauty sense, but as a source of income. The ham of a black pig is worth its weight in gold and revered as a delicacy the world over, selling at many times the price of a white pig ham.

Don Perito had always loved watching the black pigs foraging underneath his tree. As a child he had sometimes dropped down onto the ground in the early mornings and taken a ride on the back of one of these strong creatures, galloping across the grass and shouting with glee. He had forgotten the times a pig had thrown him off and left him bruised and battered, leaving him to limp back to his tree before the world woke up completely and he had to stay hidden until sundown.

That faithful day when he had been expelled, had started as most days did. The difference was that below his tree lay yet another dead and broken black pig. Don Perito had not noticed that he had grown larger and heavier as time went by, just like the black pigs below his tree. The difference was that as the pigs grew, they were taken away for slaughter and new smaller ones found their way to forage below this particular tree. Being more daring as he grew older, he had practiced dropping out of the branches and straight onto the back of whichever pig was below. As long as the difference in size between the pig and the rider was not too big, it worked. But the day soon came when the weight of Don Perito would be too much for the pig he landed on. In the beginning, the pig just collapsed, throwing him off and no real harm was done. But as the pig grew stronger, it took the weight but its legs would break at the sudden landing of Don Perito on its back.

Normally the pig would drag itself away from where it had been attacked, screaming and whimpering as it went. As this happened more frequently, the landowner became more vigilant and soon homed in on a particular area where these unexplained attacks were occurring. The death or injury of a black pig caused a great financial shortfall in this very competitive business. A dead or injured pig could not be certified as genuine because the meat had been subjected to extreme strain which would show up in the curing process.

On this particular day, as the dead pig is still lying underneath the Holm Oak where Don Perito lives with his parents and relatives, the Landowner has been summoned by a laborer, looks up into the branches and shouts at the tree that if this killing does not stop, he will cut down the tree. As if he knows there is somebody up there, he shakes his fist and announces that if another dead or injured pig is found anywhere near or under this particular tree, he will not hesitate to lose a valuable source of food for his precious pigs. This Holm Oak will be cut down.

There is a sudden rustle of leaves in the branches, even though it is a day without any wind.

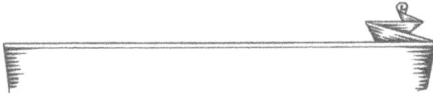

# Chapter 10: Donna has to decide

There are no volunteers. How could there be? The four Elders and Donna are still sitting on their branches, unsure as to how they should tackle this unprecedented situation. Neither of the five is inclined to believe the situation is real. Where did this person come from, what is his background, and what right has he got to throw his weight about?

Some investigation has to be done, and done quickly. But who can they trust? Who do they ask about this stranger? He has to have come from somewhere close by, to have picked up so many details about life in this beautiful row of Holm Oaks.

Thinking about the family dispelled earlier in the year, and the malevolence of the woman who had been made to leave with her henpecked husband and her misbehaved brood, Donna concludes that this stranger now threatening their existence must have spent time in the clump of trees downhill from this village. That is where he has picked up detailed knowledge that he is now trying to use to take over her position and force the demise of one of her Elder friends.

Remembering the young boy she had spotted earlier in the year looking up at her tree one night, she gets a strange feeling that something unusual might be about to happen. Looking down onto the pavement, hoping to spot the boy there, she is disappointed. There is no one anywhere; all is quiet at this time of night.

Donna explains to her Elders about the boy and how he had invoked a sense of peace and comfort in her, even though no words had been exchanged. He seemed to have the gift of transcending between the two worlds they live in.

Pepe, who is the oldest and has seen more than most, is not surprised. He can recall stories of similar happenings though long before his time and of course not in this row of Holm Oaks; they are not much older than Pepe himself.

There is not much of a story that Pepe can tell, memory fading over the years. Enough remains though that he feels confident that the boy mentioned will be able to help them in their present crisis. The question is how to contact him and in time to defeat the imposter lurking in Tree Number Nine, not that far from where they are sitting at the moment.

Donna is relieved that they are moving to a state of defiance and not a state of acceptance. She announces an end to the meeting with a promise to keep an eye out for the boy and in the meantime she will challenge Don Perito to explain as to how he comes to be in her row of Holm Oaks in the first place. Uninvited!

# Chapter 11: Don Perito leaves home

It only takes a few minutes for the parents and relatives of Don Perito to decide that he has to go.

Defiant he leaves the nest, so to speak. Already far too big to stay at home anyway he drops down late in the night without landing on a pig and sets out towards the coming sunrise. He is a tall handsome lad but with a distinct mean streak and an air about him that stinks of hard done by. Undeservedly he thinks.

He has no problem wandering the countryside unobserved, firstly because the initial part of his eastward journey is across the vast fields of the unfriendly landowner. Secondly because of his ability as a Tree Dweller to avoid being remembered by whomever he might meet.

He cannot resist though kicking a few black pigs before he leaves the domain of his birth.

Deciding to take a south-easterly track, towards the lush Andalusian cork oak woods he has heard of, he walks on, night after night. Resting in all sorts of trees along the way he manages to survive. Not all trees attract birds for nighttime roosting so food is not always forthcoming. Quite often hungry and nearly always angry, his mind festers with the thought of revenge. Against whom he is not sure, but the rage keeps him going.

At some point, many weeks and months after he was forced to leave home, he arrives in a wooded area with lakes and hills which looks very inviting. The problem though, the trees are of the pine family and not at all friendly or useful to Tree Dwellers. He is forced to rest in small caves sleeping on the ground. This experience keeps the glow of his anger alight and he is determined to find a friendlier place for himself.

Pressing on, to get through this unfriendly part of the country, he eventually reaches open spaces and fresh air again. The hills are pleasantly undulating and the terrain leads downwards to a faraway river valley.

That is when he spots a small clump of Holm Oaks on a hillside overlooking a slow-flowing river. The area of the riverbanks is covered in large orchards of orange, lemon, and olive trees. He does not doubt that he has arrived at his chosen rightful destination.

Approaching the Holm Oak cluster, he waits until nightfall and then knocks on a trunk. Asking for shelter for the night, he is invited up into the branches and offered to take part in the evening meal of sparrows and starlings arriving to roost for the night.

# Chapter 12: Donna and Don Perito

The new moon night is fast approaching and little time is left to sort out the issue of Don Perito having had the audacity to challenge Donna's authority.

A meeting is arranged just between the imposter and herself on the last night before the New Moon, two nights hence. There will be just the two of them, Donna feeling confident that her opponent will not resort to violence but will use words of reason and persuasion to get his demands met.

When Don Perito arrives, Donna makes sure she has the highest branch and only the lowest branch is available for her visitor, the other branches are covered in various objects making them out of bounds.

Taller than Donna, Don Perito is not intimidated by the lower branch offered to him. He settles in and offers her his sweetest and most insincere smile. "So, Donna, who is it to be? Who will let you have his place on the Elder Council?"

Looking at her guest with an amused smile that makes Don Perito shiver, Donna lets him know that nobody will give up their Elder seat for her. They have all refused to be replaced by crumbling. That leaves Donna to fight her position and challenge him as a leader. This she says will be a pleasure as she does not feel challenged at all by him.

Asking him to explain how he came to be here in the first place and on whose authority, she sits back and waits.

Being a clever, cunning, and accomplished liar it does not take long for Don Perito to gather his thoughts and come up with his well-rehearsed story.

He knows that to tell a believable lie, it has to be as close to the truth as possible. He starts his narration, hoping Donna will believe him.

"I grew up in the largest Holm Oak you can imagine," he begins. "It was at least two hundred years old and housed many families in its branches. The nearest tree to ours was over a hundred meters away. Trees were spread as far as the eye could see. Black pigs roamed over the vast grassy area, foraging acorns from our tree and from underneath all the others. One day my father, being the leader of our tribe, ordered me as the oldest son to go fill my pockets and backpack with as many acorns as I could gather. I was to go east, spreading acorns wherever the soil looked as if it could sustain a new Holm Oak tree. As I traveled, I was to visit other tribes along the way to make sure they lived by the standards expected of us Dwellers. Everywhere I went there was never a problem until I reached your row of trees." Here Don Perito stops his story to see if Donna believes him.

"And how were you to report back?" Donna is curious and hopes to catch him out. "What are your lines of communication? How would you tackle or solve a dispute and restore order as should be? What exactly are your qualifications, other than as an acorn spreader, a cheat, a liar, and an imposter? Answer me that, please."

"Come now Donna, your record as a leader is not exactly exemplary. I have been told of how you handle disputes and how you care for Dwellers who should be left to crumble."

"Ah, that is where your intimate knowledge comes from. The lowlife family was expelled because they put the existence of this Tribe in danger by refusing to live by our long-established rules. Shame on you! You have until the morning of the new moon night to vacate your tree and you never come back! You are a despicable person, not worthy of the term Tree Dweller. Furthermore, it would not surprise me if you had been expelled yourself from that big tree you talked about. That's it, you can go." Donna turns away from her guest and busies herself with other matters.

Don Perito slowly gets to his feet, unfolding his long limbs. As he crawls onto a branch of the next tree in the row, he turns and says: "I am not going! What will you do then you so-called Leader?" With that, he disappears through the leaves and into the night.

# Chapter 13: Urgent Elder Meeting

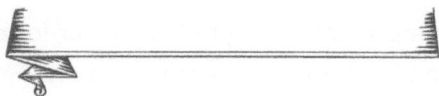

As soon as Don Perito leaves, Donna calls her Elders for an urgent meeting. Explaining what had happened, his long story re-told, filled with lies and her suspicion that they were going to have trouble evicting him from Tree Number Nine.

She would welcome any ideas and reaffirms that she will stay on as leader and that the four Elders are safe for the time being. That last is said in the hope that they between them will be able to rid the Tribe of this pest that has invaded their row of Holm Oaks.

Suggestions as to what they could do to evict their unwanted guest were few and far-fetched, with nothing remotely practical on offer.

All they can do is to wait until the morning of the New Moon and see if he has taken the hint and disappeared. Fat chance Donna thought, having had him at close hand and seen through his facade. He could be causing trouble for a long time to come.

Meeting over with, the four Elders leave to be with their families. The mood is somber though as the future sees uncertain for all of them.

While Donna settles in for the night, she casts a last glance through the leaves onto the pavement below. She is surprised but intrigued to see the young boy down there. Just standing and staring into the treetops, looking happy and content. Dressed well in a checkered shirt and blue denim jeans, his curly hair unruly but clean, he somehow fills her with hope.

Not wanting to disturb him or make contact, she stores the image among her most treasured, to be brought out for special scrutiny when she would feel the need.

Donna's mind still would not rest and let her sleep. Thoughts crowded in, each one trying to dominate the others fighting to be the most important one. Thoughts of revenge, of forgiveness, of flight or subservience kept her awake for hours. It was a huge muddle she was unable to sort out, less resolve to any degree of satisfaction. This imposter had entered her mind and would not let go. She had to win. She had to rise above this brainwashing effect.

Weighing up her options, on the plus side she had four Elders who were wise and meant well but were not fighting men. She also had a near complete Tribe whom she had treated well and with compassion during the time she had been their Leader. On the minus side, there was Don Perito in Tree Number Nine, his connection with the evicted family, and the threat or promise of the oldest son as they left for the copse down the valley.

The scales are weighted in favor of the unwanted intruder. Something drastic will have to be done, and soon.

# Chapter 14: Don Perito is up to Tricks

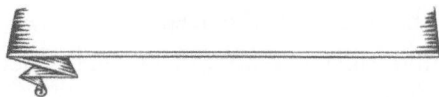

The new moon morning came and went and Don Perito is still in situ with no intentions of moving on.

He is enjoying the fact that all eyes and ears are on him and what he intends to do.

He knows what he wants to do. He wants to create havoc, he wants to make sure that Donna gives him what he wants and what in his warped mind is rightfully his: Control of twenty-three Holm Oak families. Families that will do his bidding and give him whatever he asks of them.

But first, he has to upset the way things have worked for as long as this row of Holm Oaks has been populated.

He has been told about Miguel the Street Sweeper who has a special affinity with the Dwellers, even if he has never met one. Now might be his chance.

Don Perito intends to play a few tricks on him next time he passes below Tree number Nine, going about his duties.

Miguel as usual is about early as there are many streets to sweep. He likes to be beneath the row of Holm Oaks before anyone else. He sees it as his duty to brush any crumbled dust safely off the pavement before someone walks all over it. Taking a rest below Tree Number Nine, he does not notice a long arm reaching down to grab his broom and deposit it on the ground next to his cart, first detaching the broom head from the handle.

Turning around as he thinks he heard a quiet giggle, Miguel looks first at his cart and then up into the tree above him. Disturbed, he looks further around and eventually discovers his dismantled broom. "What the..." he mutters to himself. Never in his whole street-sweeping life has he had anything like this happen to him.

Don Perito is enjoying himself. While he is watching, he has been manipulating a handful of leaves, mixing in a large amount of ants and aphids that are always present. This has produced a lump of gluey substance which he now drops behind Miguel for him to step on when he bends to retrieve his broom and handle. Hoping his plan will work, Don Perito watches as Miguel takes a step back, and the heel of his boot flattens the ball of glue now sticking firmly to both pavement and boot. Miguel has not noticed this latest devious trick and moving forward, stumbles as his one leg will not follow orders.

Finding himself in a very embarrassing position next to his cart and luckily within reach of the broom handle, he rights himself, wriggles out of his boot, and tries to dislodge it from the sticky substance he has trod in. The glue is strong and will not give way. In the end, the heel is left behind and Miguel hobbles back to base to get his tool repaired and his dignity restored. He dares not tell anyone as to what he thinks just happened. No one would believe him.

After a brief rest and a quick visit to his home for a change of footwear, Miguel returns to work and makes his way back to where he left his heel. The glue has weakened in the morning sun and he is now able to retrieve his heel. He also picks up the now less sticky stuff that had trapped him. He wants a mate of his to examine it and see if it has commercial potential.

He will get his own back on the joker that played this trick on him!

# Chapter 15: Donna has plans

There seems little doubt that Don Perito will not leave his tree and intends to remain a thorn in Donna's side. Days have now gone by and the next Elder meeting is still three weeks away.

All seems quiet with no problems brewing apart from Donna's feeling that some evil is on its way and that she is at a loss as to how she can combat it.

She decides to have another trawl across all the trees to assess the mood of her fellow Tree Dwellers. Tree Number One to Four is occupied by her Elder friends so she starts at Tree Number Six, the one next to her up-line.

Knocking on a branch, Donna is invited to sit and soon she and the family are chatting amiably about nothing in particular. All has been quiet after they moved back down earlier in the year. Food is again plentiful and they have not seen or heard from any of their neighbors in a long time.

Bidding farewell with a reminder that if ever there is a problem, they should let her know, Donna continues to move up-line. A long day lays ahead and there are many families to visit.

When she gets to Tree Number Nine she hesitates. How to deal with Don Perito? She knocks on a branch and he sticks his smiling head out through the lush foliage. Offering his hand to help her across to his tree, she grabs it. Halfway across, he lets go and Donna falls onto a lower branch, severely shaken by this uncalled-for mischief. Laughing loudly Don Perito sits back, watching her recover and then slowly climb onto a thicker branch.

"Well that was fun, was it not?" Donna does not reply, just staring furiously at this evil imposter. She then moves on without a word and carries on to the next tree.

Knowing she has no option but to come back the same way and meet him again later when she returns to get to her tree, Donna desperately tries to come up with a plan of retaliation that will put Don Perito in his place.

The unfortunate incident that befell Miguel the Street Sweeper earlier in the week had been noticed by the family in the next tree. While they recount the happening, Donna slowly forms the beginning of an idea in her mind. Not yet sure if it will grow into an actionable and doable event, she puts it on the back burner of her mind. It will sit there and simmer until it is ready.

Moving on, she gets to Tree Number Twelve, the tree where she had permitted a net to be used for catching dinner. The net has been taken down as was promised when no longer needed. The family now appears in good health and happily welcomes Donna onto their tree.

The first small sliver of her plan now showing its head, makes Donna ask this family if they have had any problems with the inhabitant of Tree Number Nine. With a little bit of nudging, it becomes clear that Don Perito has tried to charm his way into their minds, poisoning them against Donna as a leader.

A referendum springs to mind. It is not in their rule book, but who cares about rules at the moment? Don Perito certainly does not, so why should Donna? She is in a fighting mood.

# Chapter 16: Testing the mood

As Donna moves up the line, she asks the same questions in every tree as she had asked in Tree Number Twelve. It seems that Don Perito has been very busy, trying to taint Donna's reputation and improve his own with empty promises of what he would do not if but when he takes over as leader. No mention of any election or referendum in his pitch to the Dwellers.

On reaching the last tree in the line, the family greets her with open arms. The four grown-up boys are still looking after their parents and they now have a branch each following the crumbling of the grandfather.

Donna again repeats what she has said to all the other Dwellers, namely her concerns regarding the imposter Don Perito in Tree Number Nine. The youngsters offer to escort her back to her tree so she can pass unhindered down the line. They are all fired up with silent rage at the imposter and are spoiling for a fight.

Reaching Tree Number Nine, the five of them stop and listen. Is the imposter in his tree or is he out spreading mischief? They cannot hear anything. As they have not met him on the way down the line, he might be at Donna's tree creating all sorts of harm.

Deciding to investigate if he is in his tree, they enter without knocking. Nobody there! All looks reasonably tidy for a male living on his own. They have a quick look throughout but find nothing incriminating. So they proceed onward to Donna's tree.

And there he is, rummaging through her things with not a care in the world. The four youngsters jump on him and pin him down. They threaten to throw him down onto the pavement unless he promises to leave their world voluntarily.

Donna happens to look down onto the pavement then and there is the boy looking up. The boy she has given the name Boy Antonio.

Things stand still; the youngsters pinning Don Perito down appear frozen in their action. Don Perito himself has not moved since he was overpowered.

The Boy Antonio is just looking up at them, not moving but he appears serene and happy just standing and looking.

How long this goes on, nobody is aware. The power of the moment slowly dissipates and the struggle between the youngsters and the imposter continues.

# Chapter 17: The Boy Antonio

The Boy Antonio does not know he has special powers. He does not know he can make time appear to stand still. He does not think it strange that he likes to stand staring up into trees at night. He is just happy doing it. Not every night, but sometimes he feels drawn to this particular part of his village. He will sneak out of his parent's house and walk down to his favorite spot on the pedestrian crossing. From there he has a good view of the fifth tree in the line of twenty-four Holm Oaks.

He has on occasion caught a glimpse of the lady who lives in that tree. She is beautiful he thinks, with her long curly dark brown hair and round glasses. Antonio does not think it is strange that people live in these trees. It is a secret that he is not prepared to share with anyone. Well, maybe with Miguel, the street sweeper whom he sees on occasion resting beneath the row of trees.

On this particular night, he senses that something violent is about to happen. Nothing is moving though in Tree Number Five. He can see several Dwellers up there but they look frozen in time. As The Boy Antonio relaxes, the time starts to move again, but slowly. The four youngsters have a good grip on Don Perito who has also started to move. Donna shakes her head as if to clear a fog and now sees the scene in front of her. Her nemesis is pinned down, struggling to free himself.

There will never be a better time to get rid of Don Perito, but Tribe rules demand a fair hearing, even for an imposter who, if allowed to stay will cause incalculable damage.

Looking down to see if The Boy Antonio is still there, she is happy that he is. He gives her hope and courage by just looking up at her tree. She asks one of the youngsters to fetch the four Elders in a hurry. No time to waste now they have Don Perito pinned down.

Roused from their sleeping trunk or dragged away from a family meal, they soon arrive, questions abound, but they quickly comprehend the situation confronting them.

The Imposter has been caught red-handed in a tree other than his own. That is a serious breach of their rules and must be punished forthwith. It is not a kangaroo court, but a long-established way of dealing swiftly with serious offenders. Donna does not take part in the deliberations as it is her tree that has been invaded.

After only a few minutes, the four Elders announce their verdict: Immediate eviction!

Swiftly the four youngsters push Don Perito head first through the branches where he lands on the pavement at the feet of Boy Antonio.

Making the time stand still again, Boy Antonio waits for Miguel the Street Sweeper to start his day. It is after all now late into the night and his shift will start soon. It would be sweet justice if Miguel would have a chance to make a payback for the humiliation he suffered a few days ago.

After an hour, with nothing and no one moving apart from The Boy Antonio, Miguel appears with his cart and broom looking out for any piles of crumbled dust that need special reverential attention. Nothing so far, as he works his way towards Tree Number Five where he spots two bodies on the pavement, one standing and one lying prone.

The Boy Antonio waits a while keeping time still allowing Miguel to take in the scene. Not sure who the chap is, lying on the pavement and looking somewhat human in the sparse early dawn light, Miguel pokes him with his new broom, only to hit empty air. "What the..!" he mutters as he tries again to wake up this chap dressed all in green. By now The Boy Antonio has started time running again and Miguel's broom hit solid body mass. Don Perito stirs and opening his eyes becomes aware of where he is.

He finds himself in an undignified situation, lying on the pavement below Tree Number Five which he had recently invaded, only to be overpowered by four young Dwellers and then sentenced to be evicted by four Elders, Donna not playing any role in this as she was the wronged party and could not pass judgment.

Being pushed headfirst through the branches of Donna's tree had only damaged his pride, not his body, or his warped mind. Looking at Miguel, he laughs and recounts the fun he had in fooling with Miguel's broom and gluing his boot to the ground. This infuriates Miguel as he now knows who humiliated him the other morning. Giving the prone figure another good push with his broom, he tells him to leave this street and this row of Holm Oaks alone and never come back. He is not welcome and will never be welcomed back.

Looking around, Miguel cannot see The Boy Antonio anywhere. He raises his broom again and Don Perito realizes that this is not the time to stay and fight. Moving downhill towards the cluster of trees from where he came, he is followed by Miguel wheeling his cart and wielding his broom, shouting at the fleeing chap, "Don't you ever come back here or I will glue you to the pavement for everyone to walk on!"

# Chapter 18: Nearly back to normal

Days go by, and nothing is seen or heard from the exiled Don Perito. Donna keeps an eye out for The Boy Antonio but he too is absent. Miguel the Street Sweeper whistles quietly and happily to himself while reliving the sweet moment when he chased Don Perito out of the village. No one has crumbled either, so there is not much work on this stretch of pavement as the trees do not lose many leaves being evergreen.

So weeks go by and autumn is approaching. There is still no one living in Tree Number Nine and with the promise of rain and storms soon to come, it is not very likely that new Dwellers will arrive anytime soon.

It is time to prepare for winter. Secure anything loose to branches so nothing flies off and maybe lands on an innocent passerby.

Donna has been up and down her row of trees a few times since Don Perito was evicted. Everyone seems happy and no grievances have been reported. It looks like they will be having a nice quiet autumn and winter.

The oldest boy from the last tree has asked permission to move to Tree Number Nine with the girl of his dreams from a nearby tree. This request will be put to the Elders next time they meet. If they agree, the row will be completely populated and everyone can relax. There will be no room for Don Perito or any other undesirables.

The Boy Antonio is on his favorite pedestrian crossing looking up at Donna's tree. Donna has noticed that he is there when there is a possibility of trouble ahead. How he knows, she has no idea but in the past, his presence has been combined with his desire to warn the Tribe of looming trouble.

So why has The Boy Antonio started his nightly vigilance again? Is there trouble afoot? Donna wishes she could read his mind as he seems to be able to read hers.

Deciding to bring the matter of The Boy Antonio up again at the next Elder meeting where they will be deciding to allow the newly engaged couple to move into Tree Number Nine, Donna settles down to watch the young chap standing on the pedestrian crossing below her tree.

Mixed messages seem to pass through her mind. Picture of battles fought between armies. Quick flashes of her nemesis Don Perito talking animatedly with some lowlife Dweller on a hillside. She has flashes of seeing of Holm Oaks shaking violently with Dwellers dropping to the ground.

Shaking her head to rid her mind of these disturbing images she now concentrates on connecting with The Boy Antonio who is still standing with hands in pocket and staring straight at her tree. He cannot see her as the leaves hide her but she decides to part the branches and expose herself. She is greeted with a big smile as The Boy Antonio spots her. The smile soon fades though and he now looks extremely serious and worried.

Gesturing behind him and downhill, he tries to make Donna aware of the dangers coming her way.

# Chapter 19: Opposing Armies

Down the hill below the village in a clump of Holm Oaks there is this evening and night a lot of activity. Don Perito has managed to whip up all the Dwellers of this little enclave into a fighting frenzy. They have armed themselves with sticks torn of the oaks they live in and have pockets full of acorn plus a few of the infamous glue balls that had trapped Miguel the Street Sweeper to the pavement earlier in the year.

Setting out at a slow pace so everyone can catch up, they start humming quietly a war tune composed by their poet, one of their Elders.

As they walk up hill towards the village where Donna and her tribe live in a long row of Holm Oaks, they slowly increase their pace, the humming increases in volume and they now walk in step. Soon they get the rhythm and start making additional noise by beating each other's oak sticks together.

They are now in high spirit, envisioning how they will take down the hated Dwellers and occupy the complete row of twenty four Holm Oaks from where some of them were expelled recently.

Confident they will not meet with any resistance and that they will be able to just crawl up the trunks, throw down the occupants and take over, they smile at the thought that there is room for their enemies in the clump of Holm Oaks down the hill from where they had just come. It is not in their nature to kill, so just throwing the current occupants out through the branches and onto the pavement below and preventing them to reenter is enough justice for them.

As they approach Tree Number One, Don Perito calls a halt and caution silence. They want to surprise to be complete. He has explained his plan and they quietly spread up the row of trees, positioning themselves at their assigned tree. Not surprisingly, Don Perito has assigned Tree Number Five to himself; Donna's tree.

It is eerily quiet now, not even the leaves are moving.

When everyone is in position, Don Perito gives the command to scale into the trees. With a loud war cry that he had used when riding the black pigs back in his childhood, he starts to scale Tree Number Five.

# Chapter 20: Let Battle commence

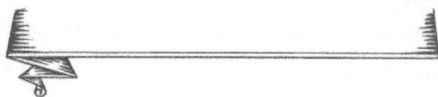

The Boy Antonio managed to convey his message of immediate danger to Donna. She in turn had summoned the Elders and after a quick meeting, they had separated and divided the task of informing and warning their fellow Dwellers of the impeding dangers.

The plan they had quickly hatched was not the best, but it would have to do. Taking five trees each, they split up and hurried through the branches. Donna stayed where she was after she had warned the families of the Elders. She was certain she would be the target of Don Perito's assault and that trees number one to four was of no interest to him.

So they waited! All had suddenly gone quiet and looking down through the branches, it was evident that each tree had a welcoming committee below, poised to attack at the signal war cry from Don Perito.

As they heard the war cry, from every tree dropped all the Dwellers living in them and landed on top of the surprised attackers about to scale their tree. The scuffle did not last long. Completely taken by surprise the attackers were overwhelmed and subdued in no time at all. Their pockets were searched and a few glue balls were found. These were used to restrain the captives to the pavement and allow the resident Dwellers to come to the aid of whoever needed it.

Donna had not dropped down onto Don Perito at the war cry. It was below her dignity to enter into a physical fight with anyone. She preferred to use her brain and mind to inflict damage on an opponent.

Sure enough, Don Perito scaled the trunk of her tree confident that his followers had done the same at their allotted trees. He did not notice that he would be the only one to succeed.

Waiting patiently on a comfortable branch, Donna welcomed her guest with a big smile. Her guest in turn looked around to see what had made her smile. He feared an ambush and was suddenly put off of his stride.

"What can I do for you Don Perito?" Donna asked politely and offered him a drink she had prepared earlier.

Don Perito accepted the drink, looking around again to try and see from where the dangers might come. A lot of his bravado had shriveled away and he did not look threatening anymore. He actually looked sad and pitiful.

Donna started to explain how she saw his current situation: All his followers had been subdued and the surprise attack had failed miserably, everyone captured, glued or knocked unconscious when Donna's Dwellers had dropped down on them. She was in control as she had always been and he was at her mercy. Soon her fellow Dwellers would come up her tree and take him away to an unknown destination. He would be stripped of his Tree Dweller capabilities and forced to live the rest of his miserable life dodging humans while crossing the country in search of somewhere to live out his days. He would not even be allowed the ability to crumble when the time came, but would be left at the mercy of animals whose job it was to keep the countryside tidy.

There was no resistance when Don Perito was grabbed and bundled down from Tree Number Five. He was allowed a look at his defeated army but averted his eyes. The captors, led by the Elders led him down the hill and out of the village. Out of sight and in the open without a safe tree in sight they performed the age old ritual of stripping him of his abilities and let him loose.

Dawn was fast approaching and the Tree Dwellers hurried back to the safety of their row of trees. They left Don Perito all alone on a bare hillside where he would face a world in full daylight that he was ill equipped to cope with.

# Chapter 21: The aftermath

The Boy Antonio had managed to warn Donna in time for The Dwellers to defend themselves against the approaching army led by Don Perito.

With Don Perito having been stripped of his Dweller abilities and left to wander the countryside there was no immediate dangers that The Boy Antonio could foresee and he soon accepted that his duties and his vigilance were no longer needed.

The morning after the attack, Donna made sure the pavement was clear of defeated and glued Downhill Dwellers. Miguel the Street Sweeper had done his best to clear away debris left from the battle and was now whistling happily to himself, having collected several glue balls that had been stuck to the pavement.

After visiting all the trees to thank her fellow Dwellers and make sure nobody had suffered any harm, she called a meeting of the Elders.

"Thank you all for coming to my aid and preparing our Tribe for battle. We had very short notice and had it not been for The Boy Antonio we might not be here now. Let us hope we can live in peace from now on, as we did before that reprehensible imposter came into our lives. Once again, thank you." Donna leaned back on her branch with a relaxing sigh.

So life went on with no other problems, other than one more Doomsday a few years later. The Elder, Pepe, crumbled on a spring night the following year and Miguel did his reverend duty sweeping the remains off the pavement. Donna was elevated to the Elder Council and the young Dweller from Tree Number Nine that had helped subdue Don Perito was elected Leader of the Tribe.

Some years later, disaster struck again, this time with serious consequences.

# Chapter 22: Irreparable Damage

The Man Antonio and Miguel the Company Director walk down the pavement that used to be lined with twenty four Holm Oaks.

Some years earlier, when it was time for the second Doomsday after the Battle of the Dweller Tribes, the local council had decided in their wisdom that pruning the row of trees was too expensive and opted for cutting them down instead. This should help balance their budget for years to come.

The first The Elders including Donna knew of the impending disaster was when they heard the chainsaw. At first, the branches were stripped naked as in the past, but then the saw attacked the branches themselves and then the trunk. Twenty three Holm Oaks left standing now.

It soon dawned on the Elders and their new leader that this was not an ordinary Doomsday event where they could bunch up and eventually return bypassing the trimming in the night.

Panic soon spread amongst the Dwellers and they demanded action from the Elders to help save their trees. After an emergency meeting, the only solution that was to be found was to flee. But where could they flee to? Holm Oaks are not plentiful in the area and most probably already occupied. Two options were discussed; downhill where the exiled Dwellers were living and uphill to the village park where a sole Holm Oak of two hundred years occupied a small grassy knoll next to bars and apartment buildings.

Whichever way they decided to take, they would be split up and forced to live among strangers. That is, if there was room for them at all. They would not be welcomed and surely resented as they arrived, distressed and with very few possessions and nothing to offer in return for hospitality.

Having lived all their lives in a community where each one mattered and help was always offered freely when needed, they would enter a hostile world they were ill equipped to cope with.

But flee they must and flee they did. Some reluctantly went downhill and some filled with hope went uphill.

Within weeks there was nothing left apart from piles of timber ready to be dragged away for either burning or to a sawmill for use in furniture or such like.

The village never knew they were there, apart from the two gentlemen walking down the pavement that day.

The Man Antonio who had helped warn Donna and her Tribe of imminent dangers was now a corpulent middle aged villager sporting a large belly and a grey pony tail.

Miguel the Company Director who had once walked beneath the trees, clearing the crumbled remains of Dweller quietly of the pavement and onto the barren ground below hoping something good would grow there, had made a fortune developing industrial strength double sided glue packs based on the Glue Balls he had collected after the Battle of the Dwellers.

They did not talk, each one lost in thought. Both missed the time when they had been of use to the Dwellers that had lived above their heads in the green leaved trees that once was a hive of activity.

The Man Antonio with his better eyesight suddenly stopped, went to the edge of the pavement and pointed.

They were standing where Tree Number Five had been and below them on the barren ground was a green shoot fighting its way into the sunlight.

# About the Author

Hans Wrang
Born in Denmark, lived 30 years in England.
Happily married to Hazel for nearly fifty years.
Both now retired and living in Andalusia since 2004
Website: www.AvellanoWeb.Net

9 798227 666093